THE ADVENTURI

ILLUSTRA

BOOK 1

A Scandal in Bohemia

By Arthur Conan Doyle

Illustrated by Sidney Paget

Annotated by George Cavendish

Solis Press

THE BOOKS IN THIS SERIES

Photo credits: cover and internal images
© Baker Street Scans/Alamy Stock Photo

This edition is based on the complete *Adventures of Sherlock Holmes* published by Solis Press in 2014 (ISBN 978-1-910146-08-8). The individual annotated stories were first published as ebooks in 2011 by Solis Press.

ISBN: 978-1-910146-50-7

Published by Solis Press, Tunbridge Wells, Kent, England

Web: www.solispress.com | *Twitter*: @SolisPress

EDITOR'S INTRODUCTION

A Scandal in Bohemia is the first of Arthur Conan Doyle's 56 short stories that were published in *The Strand Magazine* between 1891 and 1892.

Conan Doyle had introduced Sherlock Holmes, the consulting detective, in his first novel, *A Study in Scarlet* published in 1887, and then again in *The Sign of Four* published in 1890. It might be fair to say that it was not until the serialization of Conan Doyle's stories in *The Strand Magazine* that the public's imagination was caught by the accounts of Sherlock Holmes's cases. Indeed, the magazine was extremely popular at the time: circulation was at around 500,000 copies a month through to the 1930s.

In *A Scandal in Bohemia*, the first of the twelve short stories that make up *The Adventures of Sherlock Holmes*, the narrative is taken up by Dr. John Watson, who was Holmes's friend and confidant. Watson acted as an unofficial biographer, and in the story we read his account of the case.

The character of Watson was introduced in the very first book as a British army doctor who had been discharged from active duty in Afghanistan after suffering a gunshot injury. Watson was searching for a place to live in London and met Sherlock Holmes who too was in need of accommodation. They decided to share the expense of lodging in 221b Baker Street. After living in Baker Street, Watson moved away when he married. In this story he is reminiscing with his old friend.

The text is close to that as first published. I have edited some of the spellings, so that they are the ones more commonly used nowadays, otherwise the text is unaltered.

As the story was written over 120 years ago, I felt that some explanation was needed to help those readers who are not familiar with some of the phrases used by the author and his characters. Some phrases are still in use in modern-day British English, but I have attempted to describe some of these to make the text clearer to English speakers from outside of the UK, or to those who do not speak English as a first language. I have also included some background information on places, names and terms used in the story.

It is not essential to consult the notes when reading this book. However, I hope that my explanations will enhance the reader's enjoyment of this story by giving them some insights that might otherwise have been missed.

George Cavendish

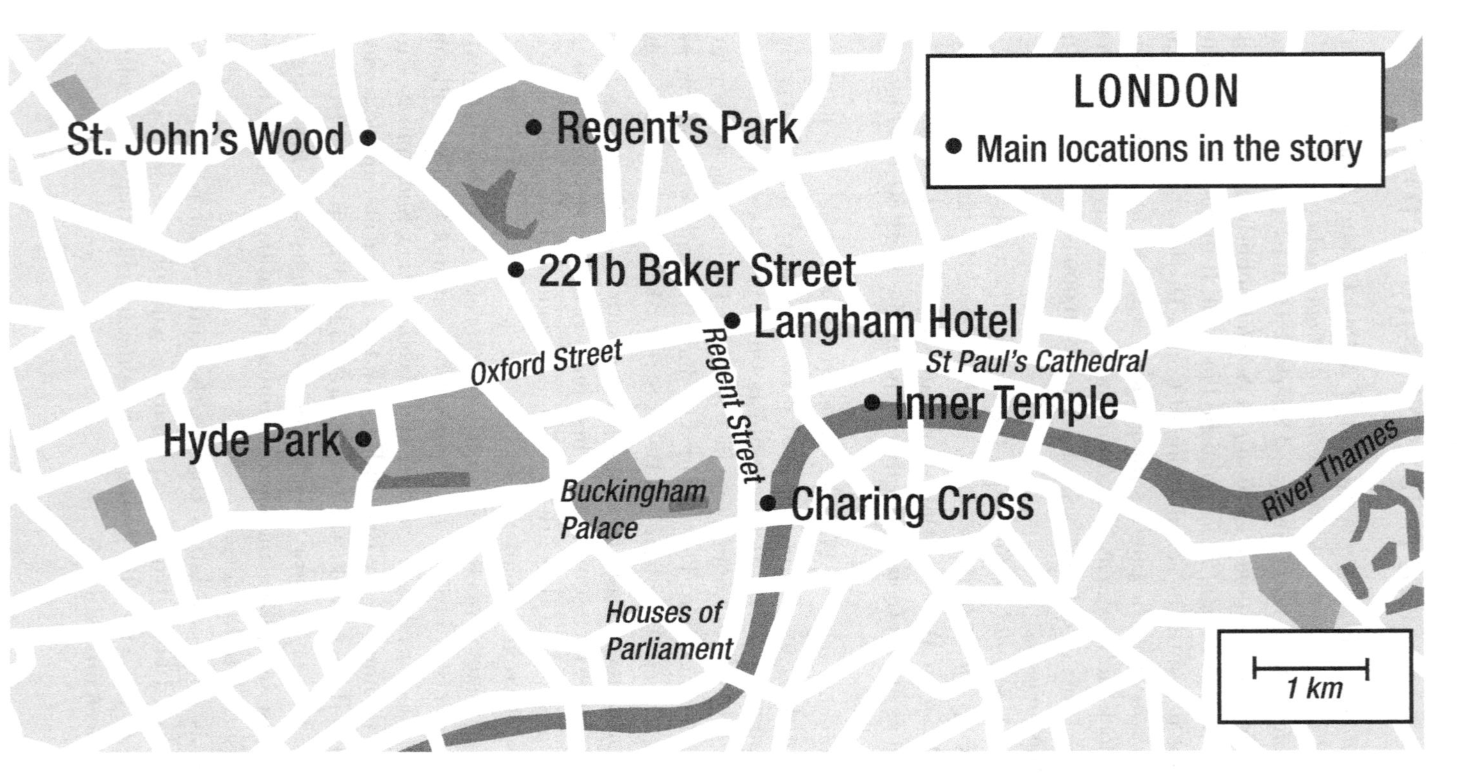
LONDON
Main locations in the story
St. John's Wood
Regent's Park
221b Baker Street
Langham Hotel
St Paul's Cathedral
Inner Temple
Oxford Street
Regent Street
Hyde Park
Buckingham Palace
Charing Cross
River Thames
Houses of Parliament
1 km

A SCANDAL IN BOHEMIA

Part I

To Sherlock Holmes she is always *the* woman. I have seldom heard him mention her under any other name. In his eyes she eclipses and predominates the whole of her sex. It was not that he felt any emotion akin to love for Irene Adler. All emotions, and that one particularly, were abhorrent to his cold, precise, but admirably balanced mind. He was, I take it, the most perfect reasoning and observing machine that the world has seen; but, as a lover, he would have placed himself in a false position. He never spoke of the softer passions, save with a gibe[1] and a sneer. They were admirable things for the observer – excellent for drawing the veil[2] from men's motives and actions. But for the trained reasoner to admit such intrusions into his own delicate and finely adjusted temperament was to introduce a distracting factor which might throw a doubt upon all his mental results. Grit in a sensitive instrument, or a crack in one of his own high-power lenses, would not be more disturbing than a strong emotion in a nature such as his. And yet there was but one woman to him, and that woman was the late[3] Irene Adler, of dubious and questionable memory.

I had seen little of Holmes lately. My marriage had drifted us away from each other. My own complete happiness, and the home-centred interests which rise up around the man who first finds himself master of his own establishment, were sufficient to absorb all my attention; while Holmes, who loathed every form of society with his whole Bohemian[4] soul, remained

1 To mock or scoff. Pronounced as "jibe".

2 To hide or obscure.

3 There is no reason to suppose that Irene Adler died, it is perhaps to reflect her former name.

4 A Bohemian is someone who rejects the "normal" rules of social conventions. The term comes from nineteenth-century France where Bohemians lived in gypsy neighbourhoods, and it was incorrectly thought that gypsies came from Bohemia. It seems unlikely that this was intended to relate to the story's title.

in our lodgings in Baker Street,[5] buried among his old books, and alternating from week to week between cocaine[6] and ambition, the drowsiness of the drug, and the fierce energy of his own keen nature. He was still, as ever, deeply attracted by the study of crime, and occupied his immense faculties and extraordinary powers of observation in following out those clues, and clearing up those mysteries, which had been abandoned as hopeless by the official police. From time to time I heard some vague account of his doings: of his summons to Odessa[7] in the case of the Trepoff murder,[8] of his clearing up of the singular tragedy of the Atkinson brothers at Trincomalee,[9] and finally of the mission which he had accomplished so delicately and successfully for the reigning family of Holland. Beyond these signs of his activity, however, which

5 Baker Street was a residential area in central London. The houses were terraced – that is built with shared walls – and made of brick. The address is 221b Baker Street. This didn't exist when the story was written, but the address was assigned in 1990 and houses the Sherlock Holmes Museum. There is no 221a: the "b" represents *bis*, the Latin for "twice". Holmes lived in an apartment attached or converted from 221. This would probably have been owned by Mrs. Hudson, Holmes's long-suffering landlady and cook.

6 Cocaine was not a controlled drug in the UK until 1916, when it was outlawed by emergency legislation introduced at the time of the First World War (1914–18). Much has been written about Holmes's drug-taking, but perhaps the last word should go to Conan Doyle's son Denis, writing in *The Lancet*, a medical journal, in January 1930: "I am writing to comment upon a recent reference in your columns concerning the character of Sherlock Holmes, the fictional creation of my father, the late Sir Arthur Conan Doyle, M.D. Your contributor's interesting notes on cocaine poisoning give the erroneous impression that Holmes was a 'drug addict.' As a matter of actual fact, my father neither conceived nor depicted Sherlock Holmes as a drug addict. He was represented as one of those rare individuals who use drugs sparingly and occasionally, and who are the masters rather than the slaves of the drug concerned. It would be superfluous for me to emphasise the differentiation between the two categories."

7 At the time, Odessa would have been the fourth largest city in Imperial Russia and an important port on the Black Sea. Now in Ukraine.

8 This case and the ones follow in the sentence are made-up cases not the subject of other Holmes stories.

9 A port on the east coast of Sri Lanka.

I merely shared with all the readers of the daily press, I knew little of my former friend and companion.[10]

One night – it was on the 20th of March, 1888[11] – I was returning from a journey to a patient (for I had now returned to civil practice[12]), when my way led me through Baker Street. As I passed the well-remembered door, which must always be associated in my mind with my wooing,[13] and with the dark incidents of the *Study in Scarlet*,[14] I was seized with a keen desire to see Holmes again, and to know how he was employing his extraordinary powers. His rooms were brilliantly lit, and, even as I looked up, I saw his tall spare figure pass twice in a dark silhouette against the blind. He was pacing the room swiftly, eagerly, with his head sunk upon his chest and his hands clasped behind him. To me, who knew his every mood and habit, his attitude and manner told their own story. He was at work again. He had risen out of his drug-created dreams and was hot upon the scent of some new problem. I rang the bell, and was shown up to the chamber which had formerly been in part my own.

His manner was not effusive. It seldom was; but he was glad, I think, to see me. With hardly a word spoken, but with a kindly eye, he waved me to an armchair, threw across his case of cigars, and indicated a spirit case and a gasogene[15] in

---

10 When Watson mentions earlier in this paragraph "from time to time", this is perhaps an understatement. For Holmes to travel to Ukraine, Sri Lanka and the Netherlands would have taken a considerable time using steam ships and steam trains.

11 A Tuesday.

12 Watson was an army doctor and now he was practising as a general practitioner, or family doctor.

13 Watson met his future wife, Mary Morstan, during one of his adventures with Holmes. (Covered in *The Sign of Four*, published in 1890 and set in 1887 or 1888.)

14 The title of the first Sherlock Holmes novel published in 1887.

15 Holmes was inviting Watson to take a drink: the spirit case would be where the liquor was kept. The decanters would have been positioned so that a handle or bar running across the stoppers could be locked if wished. A gasogene was a type of soda syphon.

the corner. Then he stood before the fire and looked me over in his singular introspective fashion.

"Wedlock suits you," he remarked. "I think, Watson,

THEN HE STOOD BEFORE THE FIRE.

that you have put on seven and a half pounds[16] since I saw you."

"Seven," I answered.

16 About 3.5 kilograms.

"Indeed, I should have thought a little more. Just a trifle more, I fancy, Watson. And in practice again, I observe. You did not tell me that you intended to go into harness."[17]

"Then, how do you know?"

"I see it, I deduce it. How do I know that you have been getting yourself very wet lately, and that you have a most clumsy and careless servant girl?"

"My dear Holmes," said I, "this is too much. You would certainly have been burned, had you lived a few centuries ago.[18] It is true that I had a country walk on Thursday and came home in a dreadful mess; but, as I have changed my clothes, I can't imagine how you deduce it. As to Mary Jane,[19] she is incorrigible, and my wife has given her notice;[20] but there again I fail to see how you work it out."

He chuckled to himself and rubbed his long nervous hands together.

"It is simplicity itself," said he; "my eyes tell me that on the inside of your left shoe, just where the firelight strikes it, the leather is scored by six almost parallel cuts. Obviously they have been caused by someone who has very carelessly scraped round the edges of the sole in order to remove crusted mud from it. Hence, you see, my double deduction that you had been out in vile weather, and that you had a particularly malignant boot-slitting specimen of the London slavey.[21] As to your practice, if a gentleman walks into my rooms smelling of iodoform,[22] with a black mark of nitrate of silver[23] upon his right forefinger, and a bulge on the side of his top-hat to show where he has secreted his stethoscope, I must be dull indeed,

---

17 That is, to get a job.

18 Watson is referring to the fact Holmes's powers would have been mistaken as witchcraft in the past. Witches were burned at a stake.

19 An informal name for a servant girl.

20 That is, notice to leave their employment.

21 Slavey was another informal name for a servant girl.

22 A disinfectant liquid that was used in medicine.

23 Silver nitrate was used in medicine as an antiseptic.

if I do not pronounce him to be an active member of the medical profession."

I could not help laughing at the ease with which he explained his process of deduction. "When I hear you give your reasons," I remarked, "the thing always appears to me to be so ridiculously simple that I could easily do it myself, though at each successive instance of your reasoning I am baffled until you explain your process. And yet I believe that my eyes are as good as yours."

"Quite so," he answered, lighting a cigarette, and throwing himself down into an armchair. "You see, but you do not observe. The distinction is clear. For example, you have frequently seen the steps which lead up from the hall to this room."

"Frequently."

"How often?"

"Well, some hundreds of times."

"Then how many are there?"

"How many! I don't know."

"Quite so! You have not observed. And yet you have seen. That is just my point. Now, I know that there are seventeen steps, because I have both seen and observed. By the way, since you are interested in these little problems, and since you are good enough to chronicle[24] one or two of my trifling experiences, you may be interested in this." He threw over a sheet of thick, pink-tinted notepaper which had been lying open upon the table. "It came by the last post,"[25] said he. "Read it aloud."

The note was undated, and without either signature or address.

24 To write down for publication.

25 At the time, London would have had up to six postal deliveries a day. The final delivery would, perhaps, have been posted at 6p.m. and delivered up to 8p.m. that same day. (Although we shall see that Holmes's letter arrived before 7.45p.m.)

"There will call upon you tonight, at a quarter to eight o'clock," it said, "a gentleman who desires to consult you upon a matter of the very deepest moment. Your recent services to one of the royal houses of Europe have shown that you are one who may safely be trusted with matters which are of an importance which can hardly be exaggerated. This account of you we have from all quarters received. Be in your chamber then at that hour, and do not take it amiss if your visitor wear a mask."

"This is indeed a mystery," I remarked. "What do you imagine that it means?"

I CAREFULLY EXAMINED THE WRITING.

"I have no data yet. It is a capital mistake to theorize before one has data. Insensibly one begins to twist facts to suit theories, instead of theories to suit facts. But the note itself. What do you deduce from it?"

I carefully examined the writing, and the paper upon which it was written.

"The man who wrote it was presumably well to do," I remarked, endeavouring to imitate my companion's processes. "Such paper could not be bought under half a crown a packet.[26] It is peculiarly strong and stiff."

"Peculiar – that is the very word," said Holmes. "It is not an English paper at all. Hold it up to the light."

I did so, and saw a large *E* with a small *g*, a *P*, and a large *G* with a small *t* woven into the texture of the paper.

"What do you make of that?" asked Holmes.

"The name of the maker, no doubt; or his monogram, rather."

"Not at all. The *G* with the small *t* stands for '*Gesellschaft*,' which is the German for 'Company.' It is a customary contraction like our 'Co.' *P*, of course, stands for '*Papier*.' Now for the *Eg*. Let us glance at our Continental Gazetteer." He took down a heavy brown volume from his shelves. "Eglow, Eglonitz – here we are, Egria. It is in a German-speaking country – in Bohemia,[27] not far from Carlsbad.[28] 'Remarkable as being the scene of the death of Wallenstein,[29] and for its numerous glass factories and paper mills.' Ha, ha, my boy, what do you make of that?" His eyes sparkled, and he sent up a great blue triumphant cloud from his cigarette.

"The paper was made in Bohemia," I said.

26 This would have been a coin equivalent to 12.5 pence, worth about £7.50 in today's money.

27 It is now the western part of the Czech Republic, with Prague being the capital city.

28 Now Karlovy Vary in the Czech Republic. In German it is called Karlsbad, but should not be confused with the German region of the same name that lies 500 km to the west.

29 A Bohemian soldier and politician (1583–1634).

"Precisely. And the man who wrote the note is a German. Do you note the peculiar construction of the sentence – 'This account of you we have from all quarters received.' A Frenchman or Russian could not have written that. It is the German who is so uncourteous to his verbs. It only remains, therefore, to discover what is wanted by this German who writes upon Bohemian paper, and prefers wearing a mask to showing his face. And here he comes, if I am not mistaken, to resolve all our doubts."

As he spoke there was the sharp sound of horses' hoofs and grating wheels against the curb, followed by a sharp pull at the bell. Holmes whistled.

"A pair, by the sound," said he. "Yes," he continued, glancing out of the window. "A nice little brougham and a pair of beauties.[30] A hundred and fifty guineas apiece.[31] There's money in this case, Watson, if there is nothing else."

"I think that I had better go, Holmes."

"Not a bit, Doctor. Stay where you are. I am lost without my Boswell.[32] And this promises to be interesting. It would be a pity to miss it."

"But your client –"

"Never mind him. I may want your help, and so may he. Here he comes. Sit down in that armchair, Doctor, and give us your best attention."

A slow and heavy step, which had been heard upon the stairs and in the passage, paused immediately outside the door. Then there was a loud and authoritative tap.

---

30 A brougham (pronounced "brohm") was a four-wheeled carriage and, in this instance, drawn by two well-cared-for horses. Most carriages, such as a hansom cab, would have been two-wheeled and pulled by a single horse.

31 A guinea was a gold coin worth £1.05. Professionals, such as consulting detectives and doctors, tended to quote their fees in guineas. It seemed to be a little more high class than pounds. A 150 guineas is the equivalent of about £10,000 in today's money.

32 James Boswell was the biographer of Samuel Johnson, a critic, author and compiler of the *Dictionary of the English Language*. "Boswell" came to mean a companion or observer.

"Come in!" said Holmes.

A man entered who could hardly have been less than six feet six inches in height, with the chest and limbs of a Hercules.[33] His dress was rich with a richness which would, in England, be looked upon as akin to bad taste. Heavy bands of Astrakhan[34] were slashed across the sleeves and fronts of his double-breasted coat, while the deep blue cloak which was thrown over his shoulders was lined with flame-coloured silk, and secured at the neck with a brooch which consisted of a single flaming beryl.[35] Boots which extended half way up his calves, and which were trimmed at the tops with rich brown fur, completed the impression of barbaric

A MAN ENTERED.

33 Six foot six inches is nearly 2 m tall. The average height for men at the time would probably have been about five foot six inches (1.67 m). He would have appeared to be extremely tall. The reference to the Greek mythical hero adds to his stature.

34 Generally, the black fur from newborn, or even fetal, Persian or karakul lambs.

35 A type of gemstone. In its pure state it is colourless, but it is often found in green, blue, yellow, red and white colours.

opulence which was suggested by his whole appearance. He carried a broad-brimmed hat in his hand, while he wore across the upper part of his face, extending down past the cheek-bones, a black vizard mask,[36] which he had apparently adjusted that very moment, for his hand was still raised to it as he entered. From the lower part of the face he appeared to be a man of strong character, with a thick, hanging lip, and a long, straight chin suggestive of resolution pushed to the length of obstinacy.

"You had my note?" he asked, with a deep harsh voice and a strongly marked German accent. "I told you that I would call." He looked from one to the other of us, as if uncertain which to address.

"Pray take a seat," said Holmes. "This is my friend and colleague, Dr. Watson, who is occasionally good enough to help me in my cases. Whom have I the honour to address?"

"You may address me as the Count Von Kramm, a Bohemian nobleman. I understand that this gentleman, your friend, is a man of honour and discretion, whom I may trust with a matter of the most extreme importance. If not, I should much prefer to communicate with you alone."

I rose to go, but Holmes caught me by the wrist and pushed me back into my chair. "It is both, or none," said he. "You may say before this gentleman anything which you may say to me."

The Count shrugged his broad shoulders. "Then I must begin," said he, "by binding you both to absolute secrecy for two years, at the end of that time the matter will be of no importance. At present it is not too much to say that it is of such weight it may have an influence upon European history."

"I promise," said Holmes.

"And I."

---

36 A vizard is a mask that covers the eyes; rather like a cartoon bandit would wear.

"You will excuse this mask," continued our strange visitor. "The august[37] person who employs me wishes his agent to be unknown to you, and I may confess at once that the title by which I have just called myself is not exactly my own."

"I was aware of it," said Holmes dryly.

"The circumstances are of great delicacy, and every precaution has to be taken to quench what might grow to be an immense scandal and seriously compromise one of the reigning families of Europe. To speak plainly, the matter implicates the great House of Ormstein, hereditary kings of Bohemia."

"I was also aware of that," murmured Holmes, settling himself down in his armchair and closing his eyes.

Our visitor glanced with some apparent surprise at the languid, lounging figure of the man who had been no doubt depicted to him as the most incisive reasoner, and most energetic agent in Europe. Holmes slowly reopened his eyes, and looked impatiently at his gigantic client.

"If your Majesty would condescend to state your case," he remarked, "I should be better able to advise you."

The man sprang from his chair and paced up and down the room in uncontrollable agitation. Then, with a gesture of desperation, he tore the mask from his face and hurled it upon the ground. "You are right," he cried, "I am the King. Why should I attempt to conceal it?"

"Why, indeed?" murmured Holmes. "Your Majesty had not spoken before I was aware that I was addressing Wilhelm Gottsreich Sigismond von Ormstein, Grand Duke of Cassel-Felstein, and hereditary King of Bohemia."[38]

"But you can understand," said our strange visitor, sitting down once more and passing his hand over his high white

---

37 Noble or imposing.

38 This is hardly a demonstration of Holmes's supposedly feeble knowledge of politics. In the first Sherlock Holmes book, *A Study in Scarlet*, Watson outlines his friend's limits and states, among others things "Knowledge of Literature – Nothing; Knowledge of Philosophy – Nothing; Knowledge of Politics – Feeble."

HE TORE THE MASK FROM HIS FACE.

forehead, "you can understand that I am not accustomed to doing such business in my own person. Yet the matter was so delicate that I could not confide it to an agent without putting myself in his power. I have come *incognito*[39] from Prague for the purpose of consulting you."

"Then, pray consult," said Holmes, shutting his eyes once more.

"The facts are briefly these: Some five years ago, during a lengthy visit to Warsaw,[40] I made the acquaintance of the

39 In disguise, or in secret.

40 Capital city of Poland, 600 km east of Prague.

well-known adventuress,[41] Irene Adler. The name is no doubt familiar to you."

"Kindly look her up in my index, Doctor," murmured Holmes, without opening his eyes. For many years he had adopted a system of docketing all paragraphs concerning men and things, so that it was difficult to name a subject or a person on which he could not at once furnish information. In this case I found her biography sandwiched in between that of a Hebrew Rabbi and that of a staff-commander who had written a monograph upon the deep sea fishes.

"Let me see?" said Holmes. "Hum! Born in New Jersey[42] in the year 1858. *Contralto*[43] – hum! La Scala,[44] hum! *Prima donna*[45] Imperial Opera of Warsaw – yes! Retired from operatic stage – ha! Living in London – quite so! Your Majesty, as I understand, became entangled with this young person,[46] wrote her some compromising letters, and is now desirous of getting those letters back."

"Precisely so. But how –"

"Was there a secret marriage?"

"None."

"No legal papers or certificates?"

"None."

"Then I fail to follow your Majesty. If this young person should produce her letters for blackmailing or other purposes, how is she to prove their authenticity?"

"There is the writing."

41 An adventuress in this sense is a woman who schemes to win social position and wealth by unscrupulous or questionable means.

42 A state on the east coast of the USA.

43 The deepest of women's singing voices.

44 A famous opera house in Milan, Italy.

45 The leading female singer in an opera company.

46 "Young person" is an odd phrase here. Adler was thirty years old, only four years younger than Holmes. Presumably, Holmes didn't wish to refer to her as a "lady", as she was not demonstrating ladylike qualities of the higher classes, or as a "woman", as she was famous opera singer and not a working-class woman.

"Pooh, pooh![47] Forgery."

"My private notepaper."

"Stolen."

"My own seal."

"Imitated."

"My photograph."

"Bought."

"We were both in the photograph."

"Oh, dear! That is very bad! Your Majesty has indeed committed an indiscretion."

"I was mad – insane."

"You have compromised yourself seriously."

"I was only Crown Prince then. I was young. I am but thirty now."

"It must be recovered."

"We have tried and failed."

"Your Majesty must pay. It must be bought."

"She will not sell."

"Stolen, then."

"Five attempts have been made. Twice burglars in my pay ransacked her house. Once we diverted her luggage when she travelled. Twice she has been waylaid. There has been no result."

"No sign of it?"

"Absolutely none."

Holmes laughed. "It is quite a pretty little problem," said he.

"But a very serious one to me," returned the King, reproachfully.

"Very, indeed. And what does she propose to do with the photograph?"

"To ruin me."

"But how?"

"I am about to be married."

---

47 A colloquial expression of disdain or disbelief.

"So I have heard."

"To Clotilde Lothman von Saxe-Meningen, second daughter of the King of Scandinavia.[48] You may know the strict principles of her family. She is herself the very soul of delicacy. A shadow of a doubt as to my conduct would bring the matter to an end."

"And Irene Adler?"

"Threatens to send them the photograph. And she will do it. I know that she will do it. You do not know her, but she has a soul of steel. She has the face of the most beautiful of women, and the mind of the most resolute of men. Rather than I should marry another woman, there are no lengths to which she would not go – none."

"You are sure that she has not sent it yet?"

"I am sure."

"And why?"

"Because she has said that she would send it on the day when the betrothal was publicly proclaimed. That will be next Monday."

"Oh, then we have three days yet," said Holmes, with a yawn. "That is very fortunate, as I have one or two matters of importance to look into just at present. Your Majesty will, of course, stay in London for the present?"

"Certainly. You will find me at the Langham,[49] under the name of the Count Von Kramm."

"Then I shall drop you a line to let you know how we progress."

"Pray do so. I shall be all anxiety."

"Then, as to money?"

48 The king of both Sweden and Norway.

49 An upmarket hotel. It still exists: "Heads of state, celebrities and tycoons have made The Langham their choice among London luxury hotels since 1865."

"You have *carte blanche*."[50]

"Absolutely?"

"I tell you that I would give one of the provinces of my kingdom to have that photograph."

"And for present expenses?"

The King took a heavy chamois[51] leather bag from under his cloak, and laid it on the table.

"There are three hundred pounds in gold, and seven hundred in notes," he said.

Holmes scribbled a receipt upon a sheet of his notebook, and handed it to him.

"And mademoiselle's[52] address?" he asked.

"Is Briony Lodge, Serpentine Avenue, St. John's Wood."[53]

Holmes took a note of it. "One other question," said he. "Was the photograph a cabinet?"[54]

"It was."

"Then, good night, your Majesty, and I trust that we shall soon have some good news for you. And good night, Watson," he added, as the wheels of the Royal brougham rolled down the street. "If you will be good enough to call tomorrow afternoon at three o'clock, I should like to chat this little matter over with you."

---

50 The king was giving Holmes unconditional authority to do whatever he needed. The phrase comes from the French for a blank sheet of paper bearing a signature for the holder to fill in as he or she pleases.

51 Pronounced "shammy"; it is a soft, porous leather.

52 The French term for an unmarried woman. A neat turn of phrase away from "young person" used earlier.

53 A residential district near central London. It would have consisted of detached houses, rather than terraced which were more common at the time. The address is made up, however.

54 This was, at the time, a new style of photograph that was larger in size to earlier styles. It would have been about 10 cm by 14 cm and mounted on thick card.

Part II

A DRUNKEN-LOOKING GROOM.

At three o'clock precisely I was at Baker Street, but Holmes had not yet returned. The landlady informed me that he had left the house shortly after eight o'clock in the morning. I sat down beside the fire, however, with the intention of awaiting him, however long he might be. I was already deeply interested in his inquiry, for, though it was surrounded by none of the grim and strange features which were associated with the two crimes which I have already recorded,[55] still, the nature of the case and the exalted station of his client gave it a character of its own. Indeed, apart from the nature of the investigation which my friend had on hand, there was something in his masterly grasp of a situation, and his keen, incisive reasoning, which made it a pleasure to me to study

55 Watson is referring to *A Study in Scarlet* (1887) and *The Sign of Four* (1890): perhaps the author was referring to his earlier books in the hope of selling a few more copies.

his system of work, and to follow the quick, subtle methods by which he disentangled the most inextricable mysteries. So accustomed was I to his invariable success that the very possibility of his failing had ceased to enter into my head.

It was close upon four before the door opened, and a drunken-looking groom,[56] ill-kempt and side-whiskered, with an inflamed face and disreputable[57] clothes, walked into the room. Accustomed as I was to my friend's amazing powers in the use of disguises, I had to look three times before I was certain that it was indeed he. With a nod he vanished into the bedroom, whence he emerged in five minutes tweed-suited and respectable,[58] as of old. Putting his hands into his pockets, he stretched out his legs in front of the fire, and laughed heartily for some minutes.

"Well, really!" he cried, and then he choked; and laughed again until he was obliged to lie back, limp and helpless, in the chair.

"What is it?"

"It's quite too funny. I am sure you could never guess how I employed my morning, or what I ended by doing."

"I can't imagine. I suppose that you have been watching the habits, and perhaps the house, of Miss Irene Adler."

"Quite so, but the sequel was rather unusual. I will tell you, however. I left the house a little after eight o'clock this morning, in the character of a groom out of work. There is a wonderful sympathy and freemasonry[59] among horsey men. Be one of them, and you will know all that there is to know. I soon found Briony Lodge. It is a *bijou* villa,[60] with a garden at the back, but built out in front right up to the road,

---

56 A groom is someone who attends to horses.

57 Lacking respectability. In the class-conscious society of the time, respectability was a trait expected of the middle and upper classes.

58 Holmes is back in his "proper" class simply by changing clothes.

59 Rather than being a member of the order of Masons, this probably means "brotherhood".

60 A small and elegant detached house.

two storeys. Chubb lock[61] to the door. Large sitting-room on the right side, well furnished, with long windows almost to the floor, and those preposterous English window fasteners which a child could open. Behind there was nothing remarkable, save that the passage window could be reached from the top of the coach-house. I walked round it and examined it closely from every point of view, but without noting anything else of interest.

"I then lounged down the street, and found, as I expected, that there was a mews[62] in a lane which runs down by one wall of the garden. I lent the ostlers[63] a hand in rubbing down their horses, and I received in exchange twopence,[64] a glass of half-and-half,[65] two fills of shag tobacco,[66] and as much information as I could desire about Miss Adler, to say nothing of half a dozen other people in the neighbourhood in whom I was not in the least interested, but whose biographies I was compelled to listen to."

"And what of Irene Adler?" I asked.

"Oh, she has turned all the men's heads down in that part. She is the daintiest thing under a bonnet on this planet. So say the Serpentine Mews, to a man. She lives quietly, sings at concerts, drives out at five every day, and returns at seven sharp for dinner. Seldom goes out at other times, except when she sings. Has only one male visitor, but a good deal of him. He is dark, handsome, and dashing; never calls less than once a day, and often twice. He is a Mr. Godfrey Norton, of the Inner Temple.[67] See the advantages of a cabman as a

---

61 Chubb was the company that supplied the post office and prison service with locks, so it implies that the lock is of good quality.

62 A row of stables for horses.

63 Another term for people who look after horses.

64 This would have been pronounced as "tuppence".

65 This is thought to be a blend of dark and pale beers.

66 Rolling tobacco used to make cigarettes, it would have been thought of as low quality.

67 The Honourable Society of the Inner Temple, more usually called the Inner Temple, is one of the four Inns of Court in London. To be able to practise as

confidant. They had driven him home a dozen times from Serpentine Mews, and knew all about him. When I had listened to all they had to tell, I began to walk up and down near Briony Lodge once more, and to think over my plan of campaign.

"This Godfrey Norton was evidently an important factor in the matter. He was a lawyer. That sounded ominous. What was the relation between them, and what the object of his repeated visits? Was she his client, his friend, or his mistress? If the former, she had probably transferred the photograph to his keeping. If the latter, it was less likely. On the issue of this question depended whether I should continue my work at Briony Lodge, or turn my attention to the gentleman's chambers[68] in the Temple. It was a delicate point, and it widened the field of my inquiry. I fear that I bore you with these details, but I have to let you see my little difficulties, if you are to understand the situation."

"I am following you closely," I answered.

"I was still balancing the matter in my mind, when a hansom cab[69] drove up to Briony Lodge, and a gentleman sprang out. He was a remarkably handsome man, dark, aquiline,[70] and moustached – evidently the man of whom I had heard. He appeared to be in a great hurry, shouted to the cabman to wait, and brushed past the maid who opened the door with the air of a man who was thoroughly at home.

"He was in the house about half an hour, and I could catch glimpses of him, in the windows of the sitting-room, pacing up and down, talking excitedly and waving his arms. Of her I could see nothing. Presently he emerged, looking even more flurried than before. As he stepped up to the cab, he

a barrister in England and Wales, an individual must belong to one of these Inns.

68 A name for offices used by lawyers and some other professional practitioners, but also an old-fashioned word for a room.

69 A two-wheeled carriage pulled by a single horse.

70 From "eagle-like" – he had a big nose.

pulled a gold watch from his pocket and looked at it earnestly. 'Drive like the devil,' he shouted, 'first to Gross & Hankey's[71] in Regent Street, and then to the Church of St. Monica in the Edgware Road.[72] Half a guinea if you do it in twenty minutes!'

"Away they went, and I was just wondering whether I should not do well to follow them, when up the lane came a neat little landau,[73] the coachman with his coat only half buttoned, and his tie under his ear, while all the tags of his harness were sticking out of the buckles. It hadn't pulled up before she shot out of the hall door and into it. I only caught a glimpse of her at the moment, but she was a lovely woman, with a face that a man might die for.[74]

" 'The Church of St. Monica, John,' she cried, 'and half a sovereign[75] if you reach it in twenty minutes.'

"This was quite too good to lose, Watson. I was just balancing whether I should run for it, or whether I should perch behind her landau, when a cab came through the street. The driver looked twice at such a shabby fare; but I jumped in before he could object. 'The Church of St. Monica,' said I, 'and half a sovereign if you reach it in twenty minutes.' It was twenty-five minutes to twelve, and of course it was clear enough what was in the wind.[76]

"My cabby drove fast. I don't think I ever drove faster, but the others were there before us. The cab and the landau with their steaming horses were in front of the door when I arrived. I paid the man, and hurried into the church. There was not a soul there save the two whom I had followed and a

71 A made-up shop name (presumably a jewellery store). Regent's Street would, and still does, have contained many upmarket shops.

72 A made-up church name.

73 A four-wheel, lightweight, convertible carriage.

74 Watson made the point earlier that Holmes was not one to speak of "softer passions, save with a gibe or sneer", but here he seems to be smitten with Miss Adler.

75 A sovereign was gold coin with a value of £1.

76 At the time, weddings had to be performed before 12 noon.

I FOUND MYSELF MUMBLING RESPONSES.

surpliced[77] clergyman, who seemed to be expostulating[78] with them. They were all three standing in a knot in front of the altar. I lounged up the side aisle like any other idler who has

77 In this sense, dressed in clerical robes.

78 Reasoning earnestly.

dropped into a church. Suddenly, to my surprise, the three at the altar faced round to me, and Godfrey Norton came running as hard as he could towards me."

"Thank God!" he cried. "You'll do. Come! Come!"

"What then?" I asked.

"Come man, come, only three minutes, or it won't be legal."

"I was half dragged up to the altar, and, before I knew where I was, I found myself mumbling responses which were whispered in my ear, and vouching for things of which I knew nothing, and generally assisting in the secure tying up of Irene Adler, spinster, to Godfrey Norton, bachelor. It was all done in an instant, and there was the gentleman thanking me on the one side and the lady on the other, while the clergyman beamed on me in front. It was the most preposterous position in which I ever found myself in my life, and it was the thought of it that started me laughing just now. It seems that there had been some informality about their licence, that the clergyman absolutely refused to marry them without a witness of some sort, and that my lucky appearance saved the bridegroom from having to sally out[79] into the streets in search of a best man. The bride gave me a sovereign, and I mean to wear it on my watch chain in memory of the occasion."

"This is a very unexpected turn of affairs," said I; "and what then?"

"Well, I found my plans very seriously menaced. It looked as if the pair might take an immediate departure, and so necessitate very prompt and energetic measures on my part. At the church door, however, they separated, he driving back to the Temple, and she to her own house. 'I shall drive out in the Park[80] at five as usual,' she said as she left him. I heard no

79 To set out on a trip.

80 This will be one of the major London parks; either Regent's Park or Hyde Park.

more. They drove away in different directions, and I went off to make my own arrangements."

"Which are?"

"Some cold beef and a glass of beer," he answered, ringing the bell. "I have been too busy to think of food, and I am likely to be busier still this evening. By the way, Doctor, I shall want your co-operation."

"I shall be delighted."

"You don't mind breaking the law?"

"Not in the least."

"Nor running a chance of arrest?"

"Not in a good cause."

"Oh, the cause is excellent!"

"Then I am your man."

"I was sure that I might rely on you."

"But what is it you wish?"

"When Mrs. Turner[81] has brought in the tray I will make it clear to you. Now," he said, as he turned hungrily on the simple fare that our landlady had provided, "I must discuss it while I eat, for I have not much time. It is nearly five now. In two hours we must be on the scene of action. Miss Irene, or Madame,[82] rather, returns from her drive at seven. We must be at Briony Lodge to meet her."

"And what then?"

"You must leave that to me. I have already arranged what is to occur. There is only one point on which I must insist. You must not interfere, come what may. You understand?"

"I am to be neutral?"

"To do nothing whatever. There will probably be some small unpleasantness. Do not join in it. It will end in my being conveyed into the house. Four or five minutes afterwards the

---

81 There is some controversy over Mrs. Turner. Many people believe that is was an error by the author and he mean to refer to Mrs. Hudson, the landlady that appears in many of the Holmes stories.

82 The French term for a married woman.

sitting-room window will open. You are to station yourself close to that open window."

"Yes."

"You are to watch me, for I will be visible to you."

"Yes."

"And when I raise my hand – so – you will throw into the room what I give you to throw, and will, at the same time, raise the cry of fire. You quite follow me?"

"Entirely."

"It is nothing very formidable," he said, taking a long cigar-shaped roll from his pocket. "It is an ordinary plumber's smoke-rocket,[83] fitted with a cap at either end to make it self-lighting. Your task is confined to that. When you raise your cry of fire, it will be taken up by quite a number of people. You may then walk to the end of the street, and I will rejoin you in ten minutes. I hope that I have made myself clear?"

"I am to remain neutral, to get near the window, to watch you, and, at the signal, to throw in this object, then to raise the cry of fire, and to wait you at the corner of the street."

"Precisely."

"Then you may entirely rely on me."

"That is excellent. I think perhaps it is almost time that I prepare for the new *rôle*[84] I have to play."

He disappeared into his bedroom, and returned in a few minutes in the character of an amiable and simple-minded Nonconformist clergyman.[85] His broad black hat, his baggy trousers, his white tie, his sympathetic smile, and general look of peering and benevolent[86] curiosity were such as Mr. John Hare[87] alone could have equalled. It was not merely that

83 A device that created smoke and was used to test the airtightness of chimneys and flues.

84 Perhaps a deliberately theatrical use of the word "role": Holmes became an actor to play a new part.

85 A protestant minister from a church that is not the Church of England.

86 Kind and gentle.

87 A famous actor of the time.

A SIMPLE-MINDED CLERGYMAN.

Holmes changed his costume. His expression, his manner, his very soul seemed to vary with every fresh part that he assumed. The stage lost a fine actor, even as science lost an acute reasoner, when he became a specialist in crime.

It was a quarter past six when we left Baker Street, and it still wanted ten minutes to the hour when we found ourselves in Serpentine Avenue. It was already dusk, and the lamps were just being lighted[88] as we paced up and down in front of Briony Lodge, waiting for the coming of its occupant. The house was just such as I had pictured it from Sherlock Holmes's succinct description, but the locality appeared to be less private than I expected. On the contrary, for a small street in a quiet neighbourhood, it was remarkably animated. There was a group of shabbily-dressed men smoking and

88 Street lamps at the time were powered by gas and were lit by a person called a lamplighter.

laughing in a corner, a scissors grinder with his wheel,[89] two guardsmen[90] who were flirting with a nurse-girl, and several well-dressed young men who were lounging up and down with cigars in their mouths.

"You see," remarked Holmes, as we paced to and fro in front of the house, "this marriage rather simplifies matters. The photograph becomes a double-edged weapon[91] now. The chances are that she would be as averse to its being seen by Mr. Godfrey Norton, as our client is to its coming to the eyes of his Princess. Now the question is – Where are we to find the photograph?"

"Where, indeed?"

"It is most unlikely that she carries it about with her. It is cabinet size. Too large for easy concealment about a woman's dress. She knows that the King is capable of having her waylaid and searched. Two attempts of the sort have already been made. We may take it then that she does not carry it about with her."

"Where, then?"

"Her banker or her lawyer. There is that double possibility. But I am inclined to think neither. Women are naturally secretive, and they like to do their own secreting. Why should she hand it over to anyone else? She could trust her own guardianship, but she could not tell what indirect or political influence might be brought to bear upon a business man. Besides, remember that she had resolved to use it within a few days. It must be where she can lay her hands upon it. It must be in her own house."

"But it has twice been burgled."

"Pshaw![92] They did not know how to look."

---

89 A person who travels door to door, sharpening scissors and knives on a grindstone.

90 Guardsmen are soldiers serving in one of the regiments of guards.

91 An expression that is more often "a double-edged sword", that is something that works both ways.

92 A now archaic expression of contempt or impatience.

"But how will you look?"

"I will not look."

"What then?"

"I will get her to show me."

"But she will refuse."

"She will not be able to. But I hear the rumble of wheels. It is her carriage. Now carry out my orders to the letter."

As he spoke the gleam of the sidelights of a carriage came round the curve of the avenue. It was a smart little landau which rattled up to the door of Briony Lodge. As it pulled up one of the loafing men at the corner dashed forward to open the door in the hope of earning a copper,[93] but was elbowed away by another loafer who had rushed up with the same intention. A fierce quarrel broke out, which was increased by the two guardsmen, who took sides with one of the loungers, and by the scissors grinder, who was equally hot upon the other side. A blow was struck, and in an instant the lady, who had stepped from her carriage, was the centre of a little knot of flushed and struggling men who struck savagely at each other with their fists and sticks. Holmes dashed into the crowd to protect the lady; but, just as he reached her, he gave a cry and dropped to the ground, with the blood running freely down his face. At his fall the guardsmen took to their heels in one direction and the loungers in the other, while a number of better dressed people, who had watched the scuffle without taking part in it, crowded in to help the lady and to attend to the injured man. Irene Adler, as I will still call her, had hurried up the steps; but she stood at the top with her superb figure outlined against the lights of the hall, looking back into the street.

"Is the poor gentleman much hurt?" she asked.

"He is dead," cried several voices.

"No, no, there's life in him," shouted another. "But he'll be gone before you can get him to hospital."

93 A one-penny coin. So-called as it was copper coloured.

HE GAVE A CRY AND DROPPED.

"He's a brave fellow," said a woman. "They would have had the lady's purse and watch if it hadn't been for him. They were a gang, and a rough one too. Ah, he's breathing now."

"He can't lie in the street. May we bring him in, marm?"[94]

"Surely. Bring him into the sitting-room. There is a comfortable sofa. This way, please!"

Slowly and solemnly he was borne into Briony Lodge, and laid out in the principal room, while I still observed the pro-

94 Marm is a contracted version of madam.

ceedings from my post by the window. The lamps had been lit, but the blinds had not been drawn, so that I could see Holmes as he lay upon the couch. I do not know whether he was seized with compunction at that moment for the part he was playing, but I know that I never felt more heartily ashamed of myself in my life than when I saw the beautiful creature against whom I was conspiring, or the grace and kindliness with which she waited upon the injured man. And yet it would be the blackest treachery to Holmes to draw back now from the part which he had entrusted to me. I hardened my heart, and took the smoke-rocket from under my ulster.[95] After all, I thought, we are not injuring her. We are but preventing her from injuring another.

Holmes had sat up upon the couch, and I saw him motion like a man who is in need of air. A maid rushed across and threw open the window. At the same instant I saw him raise his hand, and at the signal I tossed my rocket into the room with a cry of "Fire". The word was no sooner out of my mouth than the whole crowd of spectators, well dressed and ill – gentlemen, ostlers, and servant maids – joined in a general shriek of "Fire". Thick clouds of smoke curled through the room and out at the open window. I caught a glimpse of rushing figures, and a moment later the voice of Holmes from within, assuring them that it was a false alarm. Slipping through the shouting crowd I made my way to the corner of the street, and in ten minutes was rejoiced to find my friend's arm in mine, and to get away from the scene of uproar. He walked swiftly and in silence for some few minutes, until we had turned down one of the quiet streets which lead towards the Edgware Road.

"You did it very nicely, Doctor," he remarked. "Nothing could have been better. It is all right."

"You have the photograph!"

"I know where it is."

"And how did you find out?"

95 A long, loose, heavy overcoat.

"She showed me, as I told you that she would."

"I am still in the dark."

"I do not wish to make a mystery," said he laughing. "The matter was perfectly simple. You, of course, saw that everyone in the street was an accomplice. They were all engaged for the evening."

"I guessed as much."

"Then, when the row broke out, I had a little moist red paint in the palm of my hand. I rushed forward, fell down, clapped my hand to my face, and became a piteous spectacle. It is an old trick."

"That also I could fathom."

"Then they carried me in. She was bound to have me in. What else could she do? And into her sitting-room, which was the very room which I suspected. It lay between that and her bedroom, and I was determined to see which. They laid me on a couch, I motioned for air, they were compelled to open the window, and you had your chance."

"How did that help you?"

"It was all-important. When a woman thinks that her house is on fire, her instinct is at once to rush to the thing which she values most. It is a perfectly overpowering impulse, and I have more than once taken advantage of it. In the case of the Darlington Substitution Scandal it was of use to me, and also in the Arnsworth Castle business.[96] A married woman grabs at her baby – an unmarried one reaches for her jewel box. Now it was clear to me that our lady of today had nothing in the house more precious to her than what we are in quest of. She would rush to secure it. The alarm of fire was admirably done. The smoke and shouting were enough to shake nerves of steel. She responded beautifully. The photograph is in a recess behind a sliding panel just above the right bell-pull. She was there in an instant, and I caught a glimpse of it as she half drew it out. When I cried out that it was a false alarm,

96 These are made-up cases not the subject of other Holmes stories.

she replaced it, glanced at the rocket, rushed from the room, and I have not seen her since. I rose, and, making my excuses, escaped from the house. I hesitated whether to attempt to secure the photograph at once; but the coachman had come in, and, as he was watching me narrowly, it seemed safer to wait. A little over-precipitance may ruin all."

GOOD-NIGHT, MR. SHERLOCK HOLMES.

"And now?" I asked.

"Our quest is practically finished. I shall call with the King tomorrow, and with you, if you care to come with us. We will be shown into the sitting-room to wait for the lady, but it is probable that when she comes she may find neither us nor the photograph. It might be a satisfaction to His Majesty to regain it with his own hands."

"And when will you call?"

"At eight in the morning. She will not be up, so that we shall have a clear field. Besides, we must be prompt, for this marriage may mean a complete change in her life and habits. I must wire[97] to the King without delay."

We had reached Baker Street, and had stopped at the door. He was searching his pockets for the key, when someone passing said:

"Good-night, Mister Sherlock Holmes."

There were several people on the pavement at the time, but the greeting appeared to come from a slim youth in an ulster who had hurried by.

"I've heard that voice before," said Holmes, staring down the dimly lit street. "Now, I wonder who the deuce[98] that could have been."

Part III

I slept at Baker Street that night, and we were engaged upon our toast and coffee in the morning when the King of Bohemia rushed into the room.

"You have really got it!" he cried, grasping Sherlock Holmes by either shoulder, and looking eagerly into his face.

"Not yet."

"But you have hopes?"

"I have hopes."

"Then, come. I am all impatience to be gone."

"We must have a cab."

"No, my brougham is waiting."

"Then that will simplify matters." We descended, and started off once more for Briony Lodge.

"Irene Adler is married," remarked Holmes.

"Married! When?"

"Yesterday."

"But to whom?"

"To an English lawyer named Norton."

---

97 Send a telegram.

98 Another version of "who the devil".

"But she could not love him?"

"I am in hopes that she does."

"And why in hopes?"

"Because it would spare your Majesty all fear of future annoyance. If the lady loves her husband, she does not love your Majesty. If she does not love your Majesty, there is no reason why she should interfere with your Majesty's plan."

"It is true. And yet–! Well! I wish she had been of my own station! What a queen she would have made!" He relapsed into a moody silence which was not broken, until we drew up in Serpentine Avenue.

The door of Briony Lodge was open, and an elderly woman stood upon the steps. She watched us with a sardonic eye[99] as we stepped from the brougham.

"Mr. Sherlock Holmes, I believe?" said she.

"I am Mr. Holmes," answered my companion, looking at her with a questioning and rather startled gaze.

"Indeed! My mistress told me that you were likely to call. She left this morning with her husband, by the 5.15 train from Charing Cross,[100] for the Continent."[101]

"What!" Sherlock Holmes staggered back, white with chagrin and surprise. "Do you mean that she has left England?"

"Never to return."

"And the papers?" asked the King, hoarsely. "All is lost."

"We shall see." He pushed past the servant, and rushed into the drawing-room, followed by the King and myself. The furniture was scattered about in every direction, with dismantled shelves, and open drawers, as if the lady had hurriedly ransacked them before her flight. Holmes rushed at the bell-pull, tore back a small sliding shutter, and, plunging in his hand, pulled out a photograph and a letter. The photo-

99 A mocking or scornful look.

100 A central London train station with connections to the southern coastal ports.

101 This is what British people call mainland Europe.

graph was of Irene Adler herself in evening dress, the letter was superscribed[102] to "Sherlock Holmes, Esq.[103] To be left till called for." My friend tore it open, and we all three read it together. It was dated at midnight of the preceding night, and ran in this way:

"MY DEAR MR. SHERLOCK HOLMES, – You really did it very well. You took me in completely. Until after the alarm of fire, I had not a suspicion. But then, when I found how I had betrayed myself, I began to think. I had been warned against you months ago. I had been told that, if the King employed an agent, it would certainly be you. And your address had been given me. Yet, with all this, you made me reveal what you wanted to know. Even after I became suspicious, I found it hard to think evil of such a dear, kind old clergyman. But, you know, I have been trained as an actress myself. Male costume is nothing new to me. I often take advantage of the freedom which it gives. I sent John, the coachman, to watch you, ran up stairs, got into my walking clothes, as I call them, and came down just as you departed.

"Well, I followed you to your door, and so made sure that I was really an object of interest to the celebrated Mr. Sherlock Holmes. Then I, rather imprudently, wished you good night, and started for the Temple to see my husband.

"We both thought the best resource was flight, when pursued by so formidable an antagonist; so you will find the nest empty when you call tomorrow. As to the photograph, your client may rest in peace. I love and am loved by a better man than he. The King may do what he will without hindrance from one whom he has cruelly wronged. I keep it only to safeguard myself, and to preserve a weapon which will always

---

102 Addressed.

103 Esq. is an abbreviation for Esquire. It was added to a surname when no other title was used. It was used regularly until about the 1970s by banks and so forth but is now probably archaic.

secure me from any steps which he might take in the future. I leave a photograph which he might care to possess; and I remain, dear Mr. Sherlock Holmes, very truly yours,

"IRENE NORTON, *née*[104] ADLER."

"What a woman – oh, what a woman!" cried the King of Bohemia, when we had all three read this epistle. "Did I not tell you how quick and resolute she was? Would she not have made an admirable queen? Is it not a pity that she was not on my level?"

"From what I have seen of the lady, she seems, indeed, to be on a very different level to your Majesty," said Holmes, coldly. "I am sorry that I have not been able to bring your Majesty's business to a more successful conclusion."

"On the contrary, my dear sir," cried the King. "Nothing could be more successful. I know that her word is inviolate. The photograph is now as safe as if it were in the fire."

"I am glad to hear your Majesty say so."

"I am immensely indebted to you. Pray tell me in what way I can reward you. This ring–." He slipped an emerald snake ring from his finger, and held it out upon the palm of his hand.

"Your Majesty has something which I should value even more highly," said Holmes.

"You have but to name it."

"This photograph!"

The King stared at him in amazement.

"Irene's photograph!" he cried. "Certainly, if you wish it."

"I thank your Majesty. Then there is no more to be done in the matter. I have the honour to wish you a very good morning." He bowed, and, turning away without observing the hand which the King had stretched out to him, he set off in my company for his chambers.

104 From the French "was born" to show a woman's name as it was before it was changed after marriage.

THIS PHOTOGRAPH!

And that was how a great scandal threatened to affect the kingdom of Bohemia, and how the best plans of Mr. Sherlock Holmes were beaten by a woman's wit. He used to make merry over the cleverness of women, but I have not heard him do it of late. And when he speaks of Irene Adler, or when he refers to her photograph, it is always under the honourable title of *the* woman.

Made in the USA
Las Vegas, NV
23 August 2025

26828863R00024